ALiens, Inc

Out-of-this-world Events

KELL AND THE

HORSE APPLE

PARADE

THE ALIENS, INC. SERIES

BOOK 2

KELL AND THE HORSE APPLE PARADE

By Darcy Pattison

pictures by
Rich Davis

MIMS HOUSE / LITTLE ROCK, AR

Mims House
1309 S. Broadway
Little Rock, AR 72202

www.mimshouse.com.com

Publisher's Note: This is a work of fiction. Names, characters, places, and incidents are a product of the author's imagination. Locales and public names are sometimes used for atmospheric purposes. Any resemblance to actual people, living or dead, or to businesses, companies, events, institutions, or locales is completely coincidental.

Book design © 2013 by BookDesignTemplates.com

Kell and the Horse Apple Parade/ Darcy Pattison — First Edition
Library of Congress Control Number: 2014906312
Paperback ISBN 978-1-62944-019-4
Library Paperback ISBN 978-149748-021-6
Hardcover ISBN 978-1-62944-023-1
Ebook ISBN 978-1-62944-024-8
Lexile 540L
Printed in the United States of America

Thanks to Todd Hutcheson for his help
with superheroes and superheroines.

CHAPTER

1

"Kell, we need to plan the Friends of Police parade," Mary Lee Glendale said.

I swiped a streak of red across my paper. I sat at an art table with Mary Lee and my best friend, Bree Hendricks.

Mrs. Crux, the art teacher, had shown us a painting by Alexander Calder called "Red Nose." Now, we were painting red noses.

"Will you march in the parade?" I asked.

"My dad is president of the F.O.P. That's what we call the Friends of Police, the F.O.P. I always march in the parade," Mary Lee said. "Will you?"

"No." I rubbed my right eye and stared at the Red Nose on my paper. It was a good thing she didn't ask, "Why?" She just kept talking.

"I think the parade should have superheroes and superheroines," Mary Lee said.

My family runs Aliens, Inc. which plans and puts on parties and other special events. The F.O.P. parade was in one month and this was our first time to plan a parade. We were nervous. Mom and Dad said I couldn't march because too many people would see me. That was dangerous for us.

Bree said, "The best superheroes are aliens."

I glared at Bree for even talking about aliens. She was painting a very long, very skinny red nose. Probably a red elephant nose.

Mary Lee said, "Superheroes aren't aliens."

Bree said, "Superman is from the planet of Krypton. He's an alien."

"My Dad says Krypton was a fantastic planet," I said.

"How would he know?" Mary Lee asked. "You can't really go there."

But she was wrong.

Bree looked up and grinned at me. She saw me peeling the skin off my face last week. I had to tell her the truth, the whole truth and nothing but the truth. I, Kell Smith, am an alien from the planet of Bix. No one else knows except Bree. Well, my parents know, too. And Dad really did go to Krypton before it blew up.

But I can't tell Mary Lee that.

I dipped my brush into black paint. I put a black line around the red nose. I studied the painting. Was this the nose of an elephant? Or the nose of Freddy Rubin? I looked over at Freddy and then back at my painting. I looked at the painting and then at Freddy. Yes, this was Freddy's nose!

He has brown eyes. I raised my hand. "Mrs. Crux, do we have brown paint for the eyes?"

"Yes," she said. "In the cabinet. You may get it."

Mary Lee squinted at me while she asked, "Is there silver paint, too?"

"Yes," Mrs. Crux said.

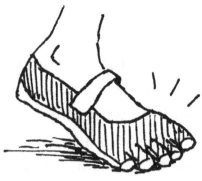

But just then, Principal Lynx came into the room. She wore barefoot shoes, the kind that shows each toe. They were sneaky shoes. She glided around, looking over the shoulders of students. When she does that, it gives me the creeps because she is an alien chaser. I don't want her to catch me.

I decided to wait to get the brown and silver paints.

Mrs. Lynx stopped behind Mary Lee and said, "I am very excited about the F.O.P. parade. It's just the sort of thing to bring out the aliens. They love to see humans making fools of themselves."

Mary Lee cocked an eye at me and then at the principal. "Mrs. Lynx, I don't think aliens will come to the parade. Just people dressed up like super-heroes and superheroines."

"Mark my words," said Mrs. Lynx. "Aliens will be sneaking around the parade. And I will catch them."

I shivered.

Mrs. Lynx turned to me. "Please thank your parents for taking on the F.O.P. parade."

"Yes, ma'am." I said.

Mrs. Edith Bumfrey had planned the F.O.P. parade for the last 23 years. But last month, a rich aunt died and left her a house in Hawaii. After she moved, the F.O.P. hired us. But if Mrs. Lynx planned to stalk aliens at the parade, maybe we shouldn't plan it. Except we needed the money.

Mrs. Lynx took a cell phone from her pocket and clicked on an app. Then she leaned over Bree's painting to see it better. "Is that an alien nose? It looks like an alien nose, and I would know."

"No, ma'am," she said. "It is an anteater nose."

Mrs. Lynx nodded solemnly. "Ah, I see that now."

There are animals that EAT ants? I didn't know that. I hate bugs of any kind. On Earth, there are more bugs than any other kind of creature. You can never tell which bugs will bite. Or sting. I made a decision: I wanted an anteater for a pet.

Just then, Mrs. Lynx's phone jingled with piano music. Her mouth made a circle, like she was trying to say the word, "Oh." Quick, she looked up and stared at Bree. She frowned and looked at the phone again and shook it.

Mrs. Crux patted Mrs. Lynx's shoulder and said, "Did you get it?"

The principal's face lit up with a big smile. "Yes. Want to see?"

When Mrs. Crux nodded, they went over to the supply cabinet and turned their backs to the class. I had to know what they were doing.

I walked to the supply cabinet and did a thing called eavesdropping. Eaves are part of a house's roof. This doesn't make sense to me. Eaves-dropping means that you listen to someone talking when they don't want you to listen. Did humans hang from rooftops and listen to other people talking?

Mrs. Lynx was saying, "—best app for finding an alien."

"Fantastic. How much did it cost?" asked Mrs. Crux.

"A fortune. But I am the President of S.A.C., the Society of Alien Chasers.

So, I got a discount. But this app didn't come cheap."

My mouth made an "Oh." I shivered. How was I going to keep away from Mrs. Lynx and her app? "What does it do when you find an alien?" asked Mrs. Crux.

Mrs. Lynx laughed. "Here's the good part. It just sounds like a ring tone. But aliens are smart. You can't just use an alien sound or alien music. Instead, it plays a cowboy song."

"I am from Australia, mate," Mrs. Crux said. "I don't know any American cowboy songs."

"Does Australia even have aliens?" Mrs. Lynx asked. "The app plays 'Home on the Range.'"

I had heard enough. I grabbed a jar of brown paint and turned to go. But I was so nervous that I slammed the cabinet door.

Mrs. Lynx whirled around and squinted at me. "Wait. Were you listening?"

My eyes got big and my hands shook. The bottle of brown paint dropped. Splat!

Brown paint splattered all over my tennis shoes.

And all over Mrs. Crux's tennis shoes.

Even Mrs. Lynx's barefoot shoes were wet with brown splotches.

"Oh, I am sorry," I cried.

Mrs. Crux shook her head at me and smiled, "No worries, mate. It's just another Accidental Art. Aja, bring us some of that paper." She pointed to large white sheets of paper.

Mrs. Crux and Mrs. Lynx and I walked all over the paper. I stayed behind Mrs. Lynx and made sure her phone never pointed at me. We made brown barefoot shoe prints and tennis shoe prints and smears. We thumbtacked the picture to the Accidental Art bulletin board. That made eleven Accidental Arts for me. But it was the first

Accidental Art for Mrs. Crux and the first for Mrs. Lynx.

After that, they went to the teacher's lounge to wash up their shoes. I washed my shoes at the sink in the art room.

"Ouch!"

I spun around to see who said that. Mary Lee stood by the supply cabinet shaking her hand and arm. "Something bit me."

Bree and Aja Dalal rushed over to Mary Lee.

"What happened?" Bree said.

"What do you mean, 'something bit you'?" Aja said.

"There!" Mary Lee pointed.

"That's nothing," Aja said. "Just a small brown spider. Hey, Kell," he called to me, "did you spill brown paint on this spider?"

"Ha, ha," I said, "Very funny."

Aja took off his shoe and slammed it against the cabinet. "It's dead now."

I was not going close to that cabinet again. Because I do not like spiders, especially biting spiders.

Just then, the bell rang and it was time to go to the next class.

On the way out, Mary Lee said, "You forgot to bring me the silver paint."

"Why did you need silver?"

"I wanted to paint an alien boy with a red nose and silver eyes," she said. Then, she slapped my shoulder and left.

Wait. How does an Earth girl know that alien boys have silver eyes?

ree is my next-door neighbor. Walking
home, I thought about what I heard
while eavesdropping. "Bree, what is a
cowboy?"

"It's a man or a boy that takes care of
cows."

I sighed in relief. "It's not a boy with
horns?"

"Nope."

Bree was used to my strange questions, so
I asked another. "Do you know a that
cowboy song, 'Home on the Range'?"

"Yes, we learned it in second grade choir.
You want me to sing it?"

I nodded.

Oh, give me a home where the buffalo roam,
Where the deer and the antelope play.
Where seldom is heard a discouraging word,
And the skies are not cloudy all day.

How often at night where the heavens are bright
With the light of the glittering stars,
Have I stood there amazed and asked as I gazed
If their glory exceeds that of ours?

Home, home on the range,
Where the deer and the antelope play,
Where seldom is heard a discouraging word,
And the skies are not cloudy all day.

That Bree, she sings as sweetly as Bix crooners, the royal birds. When she sings, it makes the sun come out and shine inside me. And I liked that cowboy song because it has a good part about the stars, and I am from the stars.

At home, Bree came over to work on homework. We found my parents in the greenhouse. Dad was dressed just in t-shirt, shorts and sandals. He knelt on the dirt beside the greenhouse wall and dug in the ground with a small shovel. Mom stood over him with her hands on her hips.

They looked up when I asked, "Can I get an anteater for a pet?"

"Where do you get one?" Mom's blue-grey eyes flashed. "We need an anteater in here."

Bree said, "Anteaters don't live around here, except in a zoo."

Dad stood and held out his shovelful of dirt. "Look. Ants and ants and ants." He carried it outside and dumped it. "Why won't the ants stay outside the greenhouse?"

"You probably can't keep them out," Bree said.

"Ouch!" Dad cried. "An ant just bit me!" And he dropped the shovel. Right on his big toe.

"Ouch!" he cried again. He jumped and danced around. He bent over and wiped his hands over his feet and legs to make sure the ants were all gone.

That's my dad. On Bix, he is a famous astro-physicist, but he can't hold on to a shovel.

When he calmed down, I told Mom and Dad about Mary Lee getting bit by a spider. Mom shook her head, "It sounds like a bad day for bugs."

"It was a bad day for aliens, too," I said. "Mrs. Lynx has a smart phone app that can find aliens." I explained about the S.A.C. and the Alien Catcher App that played the "Home on the Range" song. Bree sang it for them.

Mom frowned. "We must be very careful."

But Dad got a faraway look on his face. "Leave the Alien Catcher App to me. I can take care of it."

Fantastic. That was one thing I didn't have to worry about.

Bree reached up to a shelf and tilted a clay pot so she could look at the dirt inside. "What are you growing here, Mrs. Smith?"

"Veggies," Mom said. On Bix, she studied Bix plants; here on Earth, she is studying Earth plants.

"Oh," Bree said. "Bix vegetables."

"Yes," Mom said.

Bree looked at me. "Will I like them?"

"Some." But I was remembering how Bree hated *grawlies*, which are sort of like black French fries. They are my favorite Bix food. In fact, I wished the replicator still worked. I would make some *grawlies* right now.

Suddenly, there was a knock at the greenhouse door. Who would walk into the backyard to find the greenhouse?

In the doorway stood a policeman. Mom and Dad froze in place. And then Mom shoved Bree and me behind her.

Was the policeman coming to arrest us?

Had Mrs. Lynx figured out that we are the aliens?

"Mr. and Mrs. Smith, I hope you don't mind me coming by. I rang the doorbell, and no one answered. Mary Lee told me about your greenhouse, so I thought I'd look back here."

"Ah, Chief Glendale." Dad stepped forward and stuck out his hand. "Good to see you."

I breathed. It was just Mary Lee's dad.

"I just want to make sure you understand that the F.O.P. parade is a fund raiser," Chief Glendale said.

"Oh, yes," Mom said.

Dad nodded. "We'll raise loads of funds."

Of course, they didn't know what they were talking about. What on Earth did they know? They were aliens.

Chief Glendale pulled at his mustache. "Great. I'm glad we got that cleared up." He reached up and tilted a clay pot so he could see the dirt inside, just like Bree. "What are you growing here?"

"Veggies." Bree rolled her eyes and said, "Yummy."

"Great, great." The Chief hitched up his pants and stuck his thumbs in his pocket. "Mrs. Bumfrey took care of the parade for so many years. But I'm sure you'll do just fine.

"Oh, yes," Chief Glendale said. "One more thing. Mayor Lucky says we can't have the mounted police in the parade. He's worried about horse apples. Mrs. Bumfrey always took care of things like this. You'll need to talk to the Mayor and convince him that the F.O.P. parade must have the mounted police." Without waiting for an answer, he tipped his hat to Mom and left.

Bree said, "What are horse apples?"

No one answered.

All I could do was shake my head. We were in big trouble. Bree is the Aliens, Inc. Go-Between. That means she helps the Bix aliens understand the Earth way of doing things. If Bree didn't understand Chief Glendale, no one else would.

I am the official Go-For. I "Go for this" and "Go for that." This time, the Go-Between and the Go-For needed to get together for a Look Up Later List.

PARADE
Look UP LATER LIST

1. What is Fund Raising?
2. What are Mounted Police?
3. Why can't Mounted Police be in a Parade?

* What are Horse Apples?

PARADE LOOK UP LATER LIST

1. What if Fund Raising?
2. What are Mounted Police?
3. Why can't Mounted Police be
   in a parade?
4. What are Horse Apples?

I turned to Bree and said, "Yummy? Did you say 'Yummy'?"

She shrugged. "Some veggies are yummy."

"Which ones?"

"You know. The good ones."

Just like an Earthling girl. She won't answer a straight question.

CHAPTER 3

"Taste this."

Mrs. McGreen passed around freeze-dried string beans.

They were dry. They didn't smell green, but they tasted green.

We were in Health class and it was just three weeks before the F.O.P. Parade. Mrs. McGreen was talking about nutrition, which is what you eat. Mom says that Bixsters need to eat different things than humans eat. So I didn't listen.

Mrs. McGreen finished the lesson by saying, "To stay healthy, you need to eat right. You need lots of exercise. And you need lots of vegetables."

Then Mrs. McGreen said, "Kell, I was talking to Chief Glendale this morning when he dropped off Mary Lee at school. He tells me that your mother has a greenhouse."

I nodded.

"Does she grow vegetables?"

I nodded.

"Could our class visit her greenhouse and see her vegetables?"

On the outside, I nodded. But inside, I wanted to cry. Because we didn't have Earth vegetables in our greenhouse. Mom would have to plant some fast.

"Very good," said Mrs. McGreen. "I will call her later."

Mrs. Parrot, the science teacher, came into the health room. "Are you ready?" she asked Mrs. McGreen.

She nodded and said, "Class, we have an announcement."

Mrs. Parrot said, "Here is what you get to do. You get to try out vegetable recipes. Won't this be fantastic?"

She waited. But no one said anything.

Mrs. Parrot said, "You get to find vegetable recipes that you like. In two and a half weeks, we will have Nutrition Day!"

That meant Nutrition Day would be the same week as the F.O.P. Parade. That would be a busy week.

"You must bring samples of your favorite recipe for everyone to taste," Mrs. Parrot said. "Isn't that fantastic?"

She waited.

Bree said, "It sounds—yummy?"

I groaned.

Freddy asked, "Will there be prizes?"

"Maybe," Mrs. Parrot said. "We can try to have prizes."

Mrs. McGreen said, "We will tell you your partner now. We want you to partner with someone who has a different family life. That way, you'll get to try different foods. I wanted to work with Aja or Freddy or Bree.

Instead, I got Ting. Her grandfather came from China, which is on the other side of Earth. When we first came to Earth, we almost landed in China. Bree was working with Aja, and Freddy was working with Mario.

Mrs. Parrot said, "OK. You will sit with your partner for the rest of class. You can talk about food you want your partner to try. This is fantastic."

Ting liked to eat hamburgers and pizza, just like every other kid in third grade. But her family knew lots about eating Chinese food and eating with chopsticks.

Eating with sticks sounded fun. I didn't like Earthling forks anyway.

Ting has straight black hair and dark eyes. She said, "Your eyes are strange. Are they silver or what? Where did your parents come from?"

"They traveled around a lot," I answered the second question.

"What is your favorite food?" she asked.

I wanted to say *grawlies*, but I couldn't tell her about that.

Ting didn't wait for an answer anyway. She said, "I love cicadas on a stick."

"What is that?"

"Big brown bugs."

Oh, no! Not bugs again. "Are you serious?" I looked across the room to Bree and Aja. I bet they weren't talking about eating bugs.

"Yes. We went to China last year to visit my cousins. And I ate cicadas on a stick. And scorpions on a stick. Very good. Crunchy and salty."

Some Earthling girls have no taste.

CHAPTER 4

All that week, Dad worked on the Alien Chaser App problem. He went to Freddy's house, and his Mom played piano while Dad recorded her playing "Home on the Range." He didn't explain his plan, but I trusted him to take care of the App.

Meanwhile, one day after school, Mom drove Bree and me to City Hall.

It is a big building with a dome. That is a huge half-ball thing on top of the building. The dome was full of stained glass, all red and blue and yellow. The sunlight came through the colored glass and made the inside of City Hall look like a party.

"Where do we get a permit for a parade?" Mom asked a guard.

"Follow the signs." He pointed to an arrow that said, "Mayor's Office."

I was still looking all around City Hall when we went around the corner and I ran right into someone. We both fell in a heap. The man was bald, except his head was covered with a yellow rug or something. But my replicator would be sad to make fake hair that bad.

Mom helped us both up and said, "So sorry."

But the man stuck out his chest and stood very tall. "Do you know who I am?"

Bree spoke in a choked voice. "Mayor Lucky?"

"That's right. And this is my City Hall."

Bree frowned. "My mother is a lawyer. She says that City Hall belongs to the people."

"Yes, yes," Mayor Lucky said. "But I run City Hall."

Mom shook her head as if to say it was time to get down to business. "We were just coming to see you, Mr. Mayor. We need to ask for a parade permit."

The Mayor sighed. "It's the Friends of Police parade, right? Come this way."

He led us to a big office door. He pulled it open and let us inside. It was a big room with lots of wood and huge chairs.

When everyone was seated, the Mayor said, "What will you do about the horse apples?"

"Um," Mom said.

"I don't want poop left all over my streets."

"What?" I was confused.

"Horse apples," the Mayor said.

"You know. Horse poop."

"Oh," Bree said.

"Look," Mayor Lucky said. "I told Chief Glendale that the mounted police can be in the parade. But only if the horses wear diapers."

"Diapers?" Bree sounded shocked.

"Yes," Mayor Lucky said. "Horse diapers are bags that go under a horse's tail and it catches the horse apples. But Chief Glendale said, 'No.'"

Mom asked, "Is there any other way to take care of the horse apples?"

"Well, someone could follow along and pick up the horse apples."

Bree said, "Oh, is that all? We can make sure someone does that. It's like taking a baggie with you when you take a dog for a walk."

Mayor Lucky shrugged. Then he reached into a drawer and pulled out some papers and handed them to Mom. "Here's the application for a parade permit. If there's even one horse apple left on the parade route, I will fine you $500."

Mom flipped through the pages. "Ten pages for a parade permit?"

"That's the short form," Mayor Lucky said. "And I'll need that by tomorrow. Paperwork takes a long time."

"Yes, sir," Mom sighed. "Let's go, kids."

But Bree went up to the Mayor and held out her hand. "It was a pleasure to meet you, sir. Someday, I will be the Mayor." It sounded like her Mom's lawyer voice.

The Mayor turned around, and the yellow rug on his head tilted to the right. He reached up and straightened it out. Then he looked at Bree's hand.

He reached out and shook Bree's hand. "Always a pleasure to meet a voter," he said. And then he turned his back on her.

Bree grinned at me. And that made the sun come out and shine inside me. I was proud of her. That Bree. Someday, she was going to be a great Earthling Mayor.

CHAPTER

5

Outside City Hall, Bree said, "Kell, we need to walk home along the parade route."

A parade route means the streets where the parade will go.

"OK," I said.

Mom drove home while we walked.

We walked past City Hall toward the school.

Bree asked, "Did you decide on superheroes and superheroines for the parade?"

I showed Bree the list.

MARCHING IN THE F.O.P. PARADE LIST: SUPERHEROES AND SUPER HEROINES.

1. Spy-Dee, the girl with eight arms, three extra ones on each side. Her name is Dee. She wears boxing gloves on each hand. Ka-Powie!

2. Buggy, who wears a uniform of bugs. He commands bugs to come and cover up his body and protect him in battle. Plus, he can tell bugs to bite, sting or cover someone's nose or mouth. I didn't like this one. It was Freddy's idea. Freddy the Bug!

3. Fever, who is able to make any enemy "sick" with a touch. He might give an enemy a fever, a runny nose, or even make him vomit. Yuk!

Bree said, "This is going to be a great parade! I can't wait."

Suddenly, she stopped and pointed to

some chalk squares on the sidewalk. Grinning, she said, "Hopscotch."

Hopscotch is an old Earth game, and Bree knew how to play it really good. It is a game about hopping and jumping into squares and throwing rocks into squares.

As a Bixster, I know how to do telekinesis. That means I can use my mind to move things. I could even move myself. If I didn't hop big enough, tele-kinesis could help me land in the right square.

I could throw rocks into the right boxes.

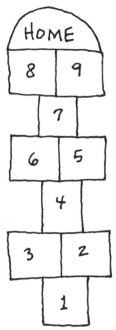

I could even make Bree's rock fall in the wrong place.

Telekinesis makes Hopscotch easy. I won three times.

After her third loss, Bree said, "It's late. I need to go home."

She did one last jump through the squares. Suddenly, she tripped and started to fall. Oh, no! I didn't want Bree to smash her nose.

Quick, I used my telekinesis and made Bree slow down. She hung over the hopscotch board for a second. Then, she softly landed on square number eight. Right where I wanted her to land.

Bree pushed up to a sitting position and twisted around to stare. "You cheated!" She stood and put her hands on her hips. "You used your alien powers to move the rocks into the right squares."

When you are caught, there is only one thing to do. I said nothing.

"Admit it," she demanded. It was that lawyer voice, just like her mom.

But I didn't want to admit anything. My jaw was shut tight. My lips were tight.

Bree shook her head. "It's not fair for you to get extra help from your alien powers. You cheated. We are not friends. And you can plan the parade all by yourself."

She stomped off toward home.

Earthling girls. Why do they have to care about being fair?

CHAPTER

K ids clattered down the steps of the bus and raced toward my house for our field trip to Mom's greenhouse. It was two weeks before the F.O.P. Parade and Nutrition Day.

We live in a 100-year-old, three-story white house. My bedroom is at the top. I can look out my window at Mom's greenhouse. Right now, all of our Bix veggies were

crowded into my room.

I helped Edgar van Dyke push his wheelchair up the driveway. Once on flat ground, he pushed it himself.

"Wow! More tree houses!" Kids who had come to Bree's birthday party at my house were surprised to see two more tree houses. That's my Dad. He misses Bix so much that he keeps building more.

Looking around, I realized that Mary Lee was absent. She had wanted to see the newest tree house. I wondered where she was.

The field trip had a bad surprise: Mrs. Lynx had come with us. She opened the door to Mom's greenhouse and called, "This way, class." She nodded to each kid as they walked past her.

Freddy pushed in line in front of me. "Bree said to tell you something."

Bree was about to step inside the greenhouse.

Freddy said, "She is weird. She said something about Mrs. Lynx and a cowboy song."

Quick, I looked up.

Uh-oh.

Mrs. Lynx was pointing her phone at kids as they walked into the greenhouse. She knew that someone in third grade was an alien and she was using the S.A. C. Alien Chaser App!

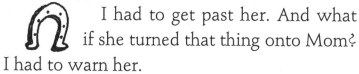 I had to get past her. And what if she turned that thing onto Mom? I had to warn her.

The kids crowded into the greenhouse, but I noticed that Edgar was hanging back. Then everyone was inside except Edgar and me.

Mrs. Lynx said, "Edgar, your wheelchair won't fit in there. You can watch from the door."

"OK. I can see from here," Edgar said.

Quick, I said, "I will stay with him. I've seen the greenhouse."

Mrs. Lynx nodded at us and stepped inside. She crept around the back of the crowd, still pointing her phone at kids.

From the door, I saw Mom beside a bench that held several pots. I tried to wave and warn her, but she didn't see me.

Mom called, "Hello!"

"Hello!" echoed the class.

Mom explained about a greenhouse. It is a heated room for plants. In the winter, a greenhouse is warm like summer. Plants love to grow in a greenhouse.

Mom bent over and tried to turn on a water hose to water the plants. But Dad had turned it off last time, and when he turns something off, it's turned off tight.

Mrs. Lynx said, "Here, let me help." She pocketed her phone and took hold of the hose.

Just then, Mom turned the handle really hard, and this time it came on. Water sprayed right into Mrs. Lynx's face.

Mom put a hand to her mouth and said, "Oh!" She pointed the hose down and turned it off.

But the kids roared with laughter.

It took a couple minutes for things to calm down. Finally, Mom took Mrs. Lynx out of the greenhouse to the deck. She went inside to get towels.

Meanwhile, Mrs. McGreen and Mrs. Parrot took over the class. One by one, they held up a pot with a vegetable plant. Kids had to guess what kind of veggie it was. Guess who knew the most? Freddy!

Freddy knew tomatoes, peppers, lettuce, and carrots. I only knew those because Mom was a botanist, a plant scientist.

When Mrs. Lynx was all dried off, she and Mom came back to the greenhouse.

Mrs. Lynx tipped a pot in the corner of the greenhouse and poked at the green leaves. "What kind of vegetable is this?"

Mom sucked in a breath. Uh-oh. It was a pot full of *shonks*, a Bix veggie. *Shonks* are like purple carrots. I eat them like candy.

"I'm not sure what that is," Mom lied. "My neighbor, Mrs. Hendricks, gave me the seeds for it, but I can't remember what she said."

Mrs. Lynx pointed her phone at the *shonks*, but it didn't play any music. I guess expensive Alien Chaser Apps can't figure out alien plants. Only alien people. Mrs. Lynx turned around to Mom again, and suddenly the phone started playing. Mrs. Lynx spun back to the *shonks*. The music stopped.

Fear stabbed through me. Mom had only heard Bree sing "Home on the Range."

She probably didn't recognize the music as the Alien Chaser App. And if Mrs. Lynx spun back around and pointed her phone at Mom, we would be caught.

Quick, I stepped into the greenhouse and bumped Mrs. Lynx's arm. Her phone

bobbled in her hands. I almost let it fall and break. But in the end, I used my telekinesis to make it hang in the air until Mrs. Lynx grabbed it.

I grabbed Mom's arm and tugged, "Mom, is it time for muffins?"

"Kell?" Mom frowned at me.

Mrs. Lynx had hold of the phone again, and her hand was shaking. "Did you see that?" she asked no one.

Oh! I had made it worse by using telekinesis. Now, Mrs. Lynx knew an alien was close by.

Mrs. Lynx started waving the phone around and turning slowly. We had to escape!

"Muffins!" I yanked Mom over the doorstep. I shoved Edgar's wheelchair into the greenhouse doorway and pulled Mom toward the house.

Mom and I rushed into the kitchen and away from that Alien Chaser App. Safe. Finally, I could explain to Mom about Mrs. Lynx and the app. I didn't want to go back out, but Mom said we had to.

On big trays, we carried out eggless Earth Bread Muffins. They are made with carrots and zucchini squash. Of course, the bread had no eggs. Bixsters are hatched, not born, so we never eat eggs. Never! And we never cook with eggs.

Mrs. Lynx put her phone into her pocket and took a muffin. Kids sat on the grass and ate and visited. Freddy and Aja and I wanted to sit in one of the tree houses to eat muffins. But Mom said, "No. Not during a field trip."

Instead, the guys sat on the deck, and we stuffed muffins into our mouths. Edgar won. He stuffed four muffins into his mouth at one time.

Mrs. McGreen and Mrs. Parrot asked Mom for the Earth Bread Muffin recipe.

And all the while, Mom and I stayed far away from Mrs. Lynx.

Then, Mrs. McGreen said we had a few minutes left before the bus came. She said, "Get with your Nutrition Day partner and talk about your project."

Ting found me and we sat with our backs to one of the tree house trees.

"Those are great muffins," Ting said. "You should bring those for the project."

"OK. And what will you bring?"

We talked about veggies and decided she would bring a Chinese green bean. "It is very spicy," she said.

I hoped it would be as spicy as *grawlies*. I said, "Just no bugs to eat!"

"Bus is here!" Mrs. Lynx called. "Line up to go back to school."

Walking back to the bus, I found Bree.

"It wasn't fair for me to use my alien powers. I cheated," I whispered. "I'm sorry."

Then Bree smiled and talked like Mrs. Crux, "No worries, mate."

And inside me, the sun came out and shone brightly. I never tell anyone about the sunshine because Earth boys don't talk much to Earth girls. I don't think they like each other.

She whispered back, "For an alien, you sure make good Earth Bread." Then she hit my shoulder and climbed the bus steps.

Wait. Why did she hit me? Earthling girls are strange.

CHAPTER 7

"**M**" "aps?" I said.

Bree held up stack of parade maps to hand out, and said, "Check."

It was after school, the week of Nutrition Day and the F.O.P. Parade. Bree and I were checking the lists and making sure we had everything ready. Dad said he had the "Home on the Range" problem solved. He didn't explain what he had done, so I was still worried. But Bree checked it off the list.

Mom and Dad were in the study trying to call home to Bix again. They've been doing that for months. The study was full of machines and wires and things that didn't work.

Bree and I had balloons to mark the route. Everyone marching in the parade knew when it started and where it started. But we still hadn't decided on fund raising. We had talked about it lots.

You can't charge people to stand in the street and watch the parade.

You can't charge people to march in the parade.

"Maybe a parade is the wrong way to raise funds," I said.

"Mrs. Bumfrey raised lots of money," Bree said. "She just had people stand around with buckets. While people watched the parade, the bucket people begged for money. But every year, the money was less and less. Chief Glendale said to try something different."

I just wanted to give up. On Bix, Mom and Dad were important. But here we have to lie low. No one should look at us or think about us, or they might find out we are aliens. But making a living is hard. Planning birthday parties is hard. Planning this parade was even harder. We might do all this work and still not make any money. I flopped onto the floor and lay there with my arms and legs all jumbled up. Nothing was going to work.

Just then, the telephone rang. Mom came out of the study to answer it. I sat up and listened to Mom talk. It was bad news.

When she hung up, Mom said, "That was Chief Glendale. Mary Lee was taken to the hospital early this morning. She has an infected arm. The doctor thinks it was a spider bite."

I swallowed hard. "It was that spider in the art cabinet!"

Bree said, "That was too small to make someone sick."

Dad stood in the study door. "In the United States, there are only two poisonous spiders. The black widow, which is black and red. And the brown recluse, which is small and brown. If it was a brown spider, it was probably a brown recluse."

I put my head on my knees and shivered.

"We need to go to the hospital to visit Mary Lee," Bree said. "She will need friends."

At that, I flopped out flat again. Hospitals were scarier than spiders. Hospitals take a long hard look at human bodies. But I have an alien body. If someone x-rayed me, they would find a *bligfa* and other surprising things.

"Yes," Mom said firmly. "Mary Lee is your friend. You must go and visit her."

"My mom can take us," Bree said. "She is out of court early today."

Mom frowned. "OK. Maybe that is a good idea."

Which meant that Mom was scared of the hospital, too.

"It will be OK, Kell," Mom said. "Just don't let them do anything weird to you."

At least I wasn't shedding my skin today.

The hospital was alarmingly big. To find Mary Lee's room, we had to walk down halls and halls and halls. And ride a big empty elevator. And walk down more halls and halls and halls. If I had to get out fast, I would be lost.

"Room 318B. Here we are," Mrs. Hendricks said. Her shoes clicked and echoed in the empty hall. When she knocked, the booming made me jump.

I whispered, "This is quieter than a library."

"That's because people are sick and need to sleep," Bree said.

Just then, the door creaked and opened.

I jumped backwards.

But Chief Glendale smiled at us and said, "Oh, it's you two. Mary Lee will be happy to see you. She's bored."

The room was small and white. White sheets on the bed, white walls, white floors. Only the chairs were blue. Mary Lee wore a strange green nightgown.

I was embarrassed. I didn't know what to say.

"Hey!" Mary Lee said. "Are we ready for the parade?"

"Yes," I said.

Mary Lee frowned. "I guess I won't get to march in the parade." She nodded toward her arms. The spider bit her left arm and it was wrapped with white bandages. But her right hand had something on it, too. And a clear plastic tube ran from her hand to a plastic bag that hung on a metal tree.

"What is that?" I asked.

"It's an IV," she said.

"Ivy? Like the vine that grows on my house?"

Chief Glendale laughed. "No. It's Intra-Venous therapy. That means a needle is in Mary Lee's vein. It is connected to the bag of medicine, so the medicine goes straight into her blood. IV medicine will make her well faster."

I didn't like this hospital room. And I didn't like the IV. I wanted to leave. But Mary Lee was a friend, and I knew my job was to cheer her up.

 I sat on the blue chair and told about Mrs. Lynx and the water hose. "I think she got water up her nose."

Mary Lee and Bree laughed, which made me smile, too. Maybe visiting a hospital wasn't so bad.

Then a nurse came in. When she saw us, she said, "Oh, I can come back later."

"No, please," Mary Ann said. "Will you show my friends your stethoscope?"

Uh-oh.

Bree said, "Yes, I want to hear my heartbeat!"

The nurse put the stethoscope in her ears and held the circle part to Bree's chest. "Yes, you are alive," she said.

She put the stethoscope into Bree's ears. Bree held the circle part to her own chest.

She closed her eyes to listen. "THUMpa, THUMpa, THUMpa."

She opened her eyes and smiled at the nurse. "Thanks!"

"You next?" the nurse asked me.

Danger! Danger! I had to think fast.

"No! Just let me listen," I said. Or did I yell it?

"You don't have to be scared. It won't hurt you," the nurse said.

"No."

The nurse shrugged, "OK."

She put the stethoscope into my ears and I held the circle to my chest. I closed my eyes to listen.

Nothing.

Silence.

I said, "THUMpa, THUMpa, THUMpa."

I opened my eyes.

Mary Lee was frowning at me. "Can I listen to your heart?"

"No!" That time, I did yell.

I handed the stethoscope back to the nurse.

And my *bligfa* hurt. I had never felt so alien. If an Earthling doctor or nurse ever tried to listen to my heartbeat, they would think I was dead. Because I didn't have a heart to beat. Would I ever get to go home to Bix?

The nurse stuck a thermometer in Mary Lee's mouth. When it beeped she took it out and said, "Back down to normal."

Chief Glendale said, "Good. We were worried last night when it was so high."

I asked Mary Lee, "Why can't you march in the parade on Saturday?"

Her dad answered first. "The doctor said no P.E. class or anything active for two weeks.

Mary Lee said, "Oh, Dad. Please! I've done the F.O.P. parade every year."

Her dad just shook his head.

But that wasn't fair. Mary Lee had done so much of the planning. She needed to be at the parade. I blurted out, "I'll think of something."

"Really?" Mary Lee's frown changed to a big grin. "You really thought of something for Bree and Freddy's birthday party. I bet you'll think of some way to get me into the parade."

"Yes, I will." I had no idea how I would do it. But I had just promised. And I keep my promises.

Parade planning was harder than I thought. Earthling girls think Bix boys have all the answers. And that wasn't good.

CHAPTER

It was Nutrition Day for the third grade. Ting brought spicy green beans and chopsticks. I baked eggless Earth Bread muffins. Bree had cheddar cheese French fries. Aja had cucumber-mint salad.

Freddy had a Caesar salad. Crazy. Who was the Caesar guy who made up this recipe? Freddy says he loves Caesar salad almost more than anything. His partner, Mario, brought pepperoni pizza. I ate two samples of pizza, but only one sample of Caesar salad.

Even Mary Lee came to school just for the Nutrition Day party. Her Dad made her ride in a wheelchair, so she wouldn't get too tired. She and Edgar were supposed to work together, but Edgar's parents never let him cook. Mary Lee did all the work herself. She brought potato-peanut butter pinwheels.

I walked all over the cafeteria tasting and tasting until my *bligfa* hurt. Mayor Lucky was the food judge. He and Mrs. Lynx walked around tasting every entry.

Then it was time for Show-and-Tell.

First, Mario was going to show about

pizza dough. He took a small ball of pizza dough and stretched it out. When it got bigger, he threw it up in the air. When he caught it, he stretched it more.

Up, down, stretch.

Up, down, stretch.

The pizza dough was as big as a dinner plate and getting bigger.

Up, down, stretch.

Mario bent his knees and threw the dough very high. It went up and up and up. But it came down behind Mario. He turned around, searching the air for the pizza dough. And it came down and down and—plop!—it fell right on top of Edgar.

Edgar had just poured a small cup of ketchup to eat a sample of Bree's French fries. Edgar whirled around his wheelchair and glared at Mario. He threw the ketchup at Mario.

He missed.

Instead, the ketchup hit Freddy's forehead and dropped down his nose. It looked just like my painting of a Red Nose!

Freddy didn't like being a Red Nose. He threw his can of Coke back at Edgar, but it hit Aja and Ting.

Someone yelled, "Food fight."

Teachers and parents tried to stop it, but they couldn't. Food flew everywhere.

Bree and I hid under a table and I protected us. If anything got close, I just turned it away with tele-kinesis while Bree cheered.

And we got to throw things at passing feet. Mrs. Lynx had ketchup on her toe shoes and Mayor Lucky had a lettuce leaf on his brown leather shoes. Pizza dough clung to the wheels of Mary Lee's wheelchair. Ting threw green beans at everyone. Freddy and Mario pretended to play baseball with my Earth muffins.

It was a fantastic mess.

Finally, Mr. Chamale, the school custodian, stood on a chair and bellowed, "STOP!"

Shocked, everyone turned to look at him. And the food fight was over.

Looking foolish and guilty, kids started picking up food and putting it on the nearest table. Bree and I came out from under the table and helped.

Mary Lee stared at Bree and me, "You didn't get any food on you?"

I shrugged, "Just lucky."

Mary Lee frowned and started to say something, but a microphone squealed.

Then over the microphone, Mrs. Lynx said, "Third grade, I am ashamed of you. You will have to clean up this mess."

Mr. Chamale got out brooms and mops. We took turns. Some kids went to the bathroom to wash their face and hands, clothes and shoes. The other kids stayed in the cafeteria to clean up. Then we swapped. I got to wash up first and then came back to mop.

The cafeteria was made of large square tiles, alternating grey and red. Each row was offset by a half square. I realized it was like a big hopscotch board.

I jumped and hopped across the floor. When she saw me, Bree hopscotched, too. And then Aja, Freddy and Ting hopscotched. Jump, hop, jump, hop. We just needed some chalk to write the numbers on the floor.

"You look like a horse galloping through a hopscotch board," Aja said.

And that was the answer. Sometimes you need to let go and be crazy. Was this one of those times? No one else had an idea. I had to solve the F.O.P. parade problems—my way. Mary Lee and Chief Glendale and Bree and the F.O.P. were all trusting me to do that, weren't they? It was hard to be crazy and brave at the same time.

I called everyone over. There was Mrs. Lynx and Mayor Lucky, Mrs. Parrot and Mrs. McGreen. Even Chief Glendale was there to pick up Mary Lee and take her home early to rest.

"Here's my big crazy idea," I said. "Horse Apple Hopscotch." I explained that if we drew big squares on the road, we could sell the squares. Each person would bet that the Horse Apples would fall into his or her square. And the F.O.P. would have a funny fundraiser.

The Mayor's head-rug had ketchup splatters, but I wasn't going to tell him that. He said, "No, you can't do Horse Apple Hopscotch. Someone will still need to clean up all that poop."

Mr. Chamale leaned against his mop. He said, "I clean up things all the time. I can clean up the Horse Apples if you pay me."

I thought about that. Aliens, Inc. needed the money, but we would be busy running the parade. We didn't have time to clean up Horse Apples. I nodded to Mr. Chamale.

Chief Glendale said, "Sure. We can pay you some of the fund raiser money."

Now everyone was happy, except Mayor Lucky. But he said, "Anything to keep the voters happy."

Mary Lee was still sad, though, because she still couldn't come to the parade. But I knew what to do about her problem, too.

"I have been reading about parades," I told Mary Lee. "Usually, there's a marshal who is the head of the parade. What if you and Edgar ride in a convertible car at the front of the parade? You will be the Marshals of the Parade."

I was afraid the Mayor would object. After all, the Mayor is often the parade marshal. But he saw Edgar's grin and Mary Lee's hopeful face and said, "As Mayor of this fantastic town, I name Edgar and Mary Lee the Parade Marshals of the F.O.P. Parade!"

It was only fair. I called, "Hurrah for Mayor Lucky!"

And everyone cheered, "Hurrah for Mayor Lucky!"

And then, everyone was happy.

After the cafeteria was clean, Mayor Lucky used the microphone to make an announcement. "The winner of the Nutrition Day contest is Mary Lee. I love peanut butter. And I love her potato-peanut butter pinwheel."

Freddy called, "Is there a prize?"

"Yes," the Mayor said. "Mary Lee wins a year's supply of broccoli from the Grocery Barn."

Everyone cheered. But not very loud.

Except Freddy who loves vegetables.

I am glad I didn't win. Edgar watched his partner, Mary Lee walk on stage, and I think he was sad that he didn't win, too. He didn't help with the potato-peanut butter pinwheels, though. So, it was fair.

Leaving the cafeteria, Bree said, "You did it again. Somehow, you always manage to sort everyone out." And she tried to hit my arm.

But this time I was ready, and I twisted away. "Too slow."

"You're learning, Earth man." Wait. Why did she call me an Earth man? She knows I am an alien.

CHAPTER 9

Getting ready for the F.O.P. Parade was a mad dash. We had to decide where to put the squares for the Horse Apple Hopscotch. We had to ask for donations for prizes. The best prize was a year of horseback riding lessons from the Davis Stables.

Next, we marked up the parade maps with Hopscotch squares. Mrs. Hendricks helped Mom organize some Moms to make phone calls and sell the Hopscotch squares. We started with just ten squares, but we kept adding more all day long. Finally, we had 100 Horse Apple Hopscotch squares sold. The fund raising was a success!

Mr. Hendricks organized some Dads to draw all the squares. They finished late in the night.

Meanwhile, Dad was still working on the "Home on the Range" problem. He was on the phone and computer all day and all night.

Saturday dawned bright and cool; it was a perfect day for a parade. Everyone gathered in Lucky City Park. At the park's center was a statue of Mayor Lucky's great-great-grandfather who had come to the area 150 years ago in a covered wagon. The statue was made of iron and painted black. But the paint was gone on his face, and his nose was red from rust. Another Red Nose!

The park was full. Chief Glendale drove up in a red convertible for the Parade Marshals. The high school band gathered under some oak trees with a rat-a-tat-tat of drums and a um-bah of tubas. Bree, Ting and the hula hoopers were near the playground practicing their routine. And little kids on tricycles careened everywhere, chased by yelling Moms or Dads.

Bree and I had hard jobs. We had to get everyone lined up in order. Bree was the official Go-Between, and she knew just how to talk with people.  Last night, we made huge cardboard numbers for each group. I was the official Go-For and walked around handing out the numbers. If anyone had questions, I was off and running, going to Mom or Dad for answers.

We alternated a superhero or superheroine with different kinds of acts. There was Spy-Dee, followed by Aja's All-Star Invisible Tambourine Band. Fever came next and had buckets of band-aids to throw to the crowd. And then came the Hula Hoopers.

I handed out all the numbers and headed back to help Bree. That's when I saw Mrs. Lynx, who wore a lime-green T-shirt that said, "Official UFO Identification." It had pictures of different kinds of Unidentified Flying Objects, or UFOs. There was a flying saucer, a space rocket, strange circles with lots of lights and more.

Mrs. Lynx's sneaky, barefoot toe-shoes were lime-green, too. But the strangest thing about her was the lime-green baseball cap. It had a helicopter blade on top. The blade had a cord that ran down to her smart phone. The helicopter blade must be an extra antenna to make the app work better.

And even worse, we saw other people dressed just like Mrs. Lynx. They were walking up and down the parade line. The S.A.C!

I had to help Bree. But I also had to stay away from the Alien Chasers.

Suddenly, right behind me, I heard that song, "Home on the Range."

I whirled around and saw Freddy punch his phone and say, "Hello."

Turning back, three Alien Chasers were running our way. But then, from over near the high school band, I heard the song again. The Alien Chasers turned and ran that way.

Confused, I waited until Freddy told his mom and dad where he was. When he hung up, I asked, "Where did you get that ring tone?"

Freddy shrugged. "My mom played the piano music. Your dad made it the official F.O.P. Parade song and ring tone. I got the email last night about it and downloaded it."

That's what Dad had been doing! The "Home on the Range" ring tone meant the

Alien Catcher App had found an alien. But now, the Alien Chasers would hear the song everywhere. The S.A.C. would chase songs everywhere and get tired when they found nothing.

But Mom, Dad and I still needed to avoid the Alien Chaser App.

Quick, I found Bree and we made a plan. I found Mom and Dad and told them the plan. It might not work, but it was the best plan we had.

Bree and I had almost everyone lined up. The parade was about to start.

If you liked bugs, you might think Freddy the Bug looked awesome. His t-shirt and sweat pants had bugs glued to them everywhere.

Tarantulas, bees, hornets, giant ticks and centipedes. Yuk. I decided to stay away from Freddy the Bug until after the parade.

The soldiers marched after Freddy the Bug. The next-to-last act was the Tricycyle Gang. Mom said to put them near the last. Once they marched, their parents would probably go home and we didn't want people to leave early.

Bringing up the rear was the Horse Apple Patrol. People who bought a Horse Apple Hopscotch square would stay for this, too.

Edgar's van pulled into the park. Chief Glendale's convertible top was already down, and Mary Lee sat on the back, letting her legs dangle onto the back seat. Mr. Van

Dyke, Edgar's Dad, carried him to the convertible and got him settled. The first car in the parade was ready!

It was time.

Bree and I walked down the parade line again, making a last check. Smiles, nervous laughs, stamping hooves.

Then, two cellphones went off at once, playing "Home on the Range." There was a black horse with red ribbons braided into its mane. The horse whinnied and pawed the ground. The policeman on his back jerked the reins up, and the horse turned around to look at him. I don't think the horse and policeman were friends.

And there, walking toward us, was Mom. She had on jeans and a white t-shirt and looked very human. No one would guess that she shed her skin once a month and was an alien from Bix. With her was Mrs. Hendricks, Bree's Mom. She wore jeans, too, but she had on a suit jacket. I guess lawyers never really relax.

Mrs. Lynx came out of the crowd and walked toward mom, saying, "Mrs. Smith, you've done an amazing job—"

Her phone started to play that cowboy song. She stopped and turned around. The song stopped. When she circled back to Mom, the song played again.

"Mrs. Smith?" Mrs. Lynx's brow and forehead wrinkled together. She looked from her phone to Mom. Then a huge smile lit up her face. And she grabbed Mom's arm and cried, "I've got you."

And Bree, my best friend on Earth, grabbed my shoulder and cried out, "Oh, no!"

CHAPTER

If I didn't act fast, Mrs. Lynx would find out that my Mom was an alien.

I was ready. Quick, I pushed the CALL button on my phone.

Mrs. Lynx's phone rang. She didn't have the "Home on the Range" ring tone. So her phone stopped the Alien Chaser App and played a boring ring tone.

Mrs. Lynx turned loose of mom's arm and answered her phone and said, "Hello?"

Just like we planned, Bree called Mom's phone, and we heard the "Home on the Range" ring tone.

I hung up on Mrs. Lynx.

Mom held her phone toward Mrs. Lynx and said, "I've got you."

"What?" Mrs. Lynx looked confused.

Mom said, "I have the Alien Chaser App, and it is going off when I point it at you."

Mrs. Lynx gave a nervous laugh. "I'm not an alien."

"Are you sure?" Mom asked sternly.

"Of course, I'm not alien. I'm the school principal." She shook her head, and the helicopter blades on her hat spun around.

"Let's just forget it," Mom said.

Confused, Mrs. Lynx nodded and stumbled away.

The switch had worked! Mom was safe. For now.

Just then, Chief Glendale beeped the horn on his convertible. He waved and called, "It's time to start."

Amazingly, the Friends of Police Parade started exactly on time.

At a parade, there is a thing

called a Grand Stand, which is bleachers where the important people sit. Mayor Lucky and other city officials sat in the Grand Stand. Mrs. Lynx and other school teachers sat there. The policemen who weren't in the parade sat there. The Grand Stands was packed.

When a parade act got to the Grand Stand, they were supposed to pause and do some kind of song or act. Bree and I made sure that each act started at the right time. When the last act, the Horse Apple Patrol left the starting point, Bree and I ran to the Grand Stand to watch. By then Mary Lee and

Edgar had finished the whole parade and were sitting in their wheelchairs beside the Grand Stand. We sat on the edge of the Grand Stand, and we all watched the rest of the parade together.

The high school band played "Home on the Range."

Then the cowboy song blared from loud speakers, and the hula hoopers whirled around and around.

Aja's All-Star Invisible Tambourine Band played "Home on the Range." Of course, I only heard Aja's tambourine and Aja singing. But soon the crowd was whistling or singing along with him. His band was a hit.

Only when the soldiers marched past the Grand Stand did the song change to "The Star Spangled Banner." That was OK. It's another song about the stars. And since I'm from the stars, I liked that.

Finally, it was time for the Tricycle Gang. The trikes were big and little, red and pink, and new and old. Some had long sticks that held flags. Others had funny sounding horns that said, "Bahooga!"

When the tricycle kids stopped at the Grand Stand, Dad passed out kazoos. They are a funny noisemaker. You just hum into a kazoo, and it sounds great. The kindergarten kids tried to hum "Home on the Range" into their kazoos, and it was a fantastic noise.

Last came the Horse Apple Patrol. The policemen wore shiny black boots and blue uniforms with shiny buttons. On their heads, they wore their police hats. The loud speakers played "Home on the Range" again and everyone watched the horses walk. When one horse lifted its tail, the crowd called, "Oh!"

And horse apples fell into Square Number 14.

I couldn't remember who had paid for that square. We would find out later when the awards were announced.

When the Horse Apple Patrol reached the Grand Stand, they all stopped and turned to face the Mayor.

The music changed. It was eerie, space music. Alien music! The policemen reached into their coat pockets and pulled out lime green sunglasses. They were just like the glasses that kids had worn at Bree's birthday party.

Mayor Lucky and everyone in the Grand Stand started laughing. Camera's flashed.

Mrs. Lynx crossed her arms and scowled. She jumped down from the Grand Stand and started to march away. The other S.A.C. people, those wearing the lime green t-shirts, started to follow her.

A horse whinnied.

More cameras flashed, and the

crowd's laughter grew louder. Were they laughing at the Society of Alien Chasers?

Suddenly, the black horse with red ribbons whinnied louder and starting skittering sideways. The policeman jerked on the rein, but that only made the horse rear up. The policeman fell. The horse dashed straight for Mrs. Lynx.

I watched in horror.

The horse thundered toward her. The principal heard the sound and turned. Her eyes widened. The horse saw her, but by then, it couldn't stop. His hooves drummed toward her.

I did what I had to do. Using telekinesis, I shoved Mrs. Lynx toward the Grand Stand. Her phone fell with a clatter. That was lucky! I used telekinesis to move it right into the horse's path. The horse thundered past her and down an empty alley.

Mrs. Lynx screeched in anger, "Someone pushed me!" Several policemen crowded around her, trying to help. But she shrank away from their alien sunglasses.

I had to help. I pushed through the blue uniforms and took Mrs. Lynx's hand and pulled her out of the crowd. "You are safe," I said.

She looked around and saw her phone on the ground. It was crushed. The horse had run over it.

Bree scooped up the broken phone pieces and handed it to Mrs. Lynx.

That made me happy. No more Alien Chaser App. Maybe we had won the battle against the S.A.C. today.

"An alien pushed me," Mrs. Lynx said. "It tried to push me in front of that runaway horse."

She glared at Bree and said, "You. My Alien Chaser App went off in art class when it was pointed at you. And I know about that strange alien plant in Mrs. Smith's greenhouse. Your mother gave her the seeds.

And now, you pushed me into the path of that runaway horse."

Bree's eyes got big, but then she grinned, "I am not an alien."

Mrs. Lynx brushed off her jeans and skirt. "I can't prove it," she said. "But someone in third grade is an alien, and I'll be watching you."

I couldn't help it. I had to ask, "Who cares if there are aliens on Earth?"

Mrs. Lynx said in her best teacher voice, "Aliens only want to take over the Earth. I will find the alien in third grade. And when I do, I'll make sure the government captures it."

I was shocked. Before, I thought this was like a game for Mrs. Lynx. But it's not. She is serious about catching aliens. She could really hurt my family. I had to make sure that she never found out about my family and Bix. But that would have to wait because the parade wasn't over.

From the loud speakers came Mayor Lucky's voice. "It's time to give out the awards for the F.O.P. Parade."

Bree and I left the principal and ran back to the front of the Grand Stand. A crowd had gathered for the awards.

"Grand Prize for the Horse Apple Hopscotch goes to Square Number 14!"

"Bonzer! I've won!" called Mrs. Crux, the art teacher. "That was a corker of a parade!"

There she was speaking Aussie again. Did she ever feel like an alien, too? I was glad she  won the horseback riding lessons, so she could learn all about American cowboys and cowgirls.

"Winner of the best act is the Tricycle Gang. Free ice cream for all the Gang!" called Mayor Lucky.

And everyone cheered. Anything to keep the voters happy, I thought.

"We did it," I told Mary Lee.

Chief Glendale was smiling. "It was the best F.O.P. parade ever."

Mary Lee said, "I'm just glad Mrs. Lynx is OK. I saw the whole thing, and I thought she was going to be hurt really bad." She tapped her hand on the arm of the wheelchair. "I think she's right. An alien—"

"Excuse me," said a man. He was the tallest Earthling I had ever seen. "Who was in charge of the parade?"

"The Smiths," Mary Lee said and pointed to Mom.

The man turned to Mom. "My name is Joel East. Do you do birthday parties? My son, Roman, will be nine soon, and he wants a giant party."

"We can do a big party," Mom said.

"No, he wants a 'giant' party. You know, something with really tall, giant people."

"Oh," Mom said.

And I thought, "Here we go again. Another Look Up Later List for another party."

Mr. Chamale and his volunteers were already cleaning up the horse apples. The mayor would be happy. Chief Glendale had to go off and talk to other policemen and help clean up things.

Edgar's dad came and took Edgar home. That just left Bree and Mary Lee and me beside the Grand Stand.

Mary Lee yawned.

"Are you tired?" I asked.

She nodded. "The spider bite medicine makes me sleepy. I should get into Dad's convertible and take a nap."

"Do you need help?" I asked.

"Yes, give me a lift, please," Mary Lee said.

I went to her chair and reached for her hand to pull her up.

But Mary Lee stared at me and said, "No. I've been watching you. You have alien silver eyes. And you wouldn't let the nurse listen to your alien heart. If you even have a heart. And you stuck out your hand to concentrate when you shoved Mrs. Lynx away from the horse. I need a lift."

So I gave Mary Lee a lift with telekinesis. She stood, and, with a little help from telekinesis, she walked over to the convertible.

She sank into the convertible seat and yawned. "Where are you from, anyway?"

"The planet Bix." It was nice to be able to tell the truth to someone else.

She leaned back and closed her eyes. Then she opened them and stared at me. "What else can you do?"

Before I could answer, Bree said, "He sheds his skin once a month."

They looked at each other and giggled. Then, together they said, "Alien boys are weird."

The End

FOR FUN

HORSESHOES ARE HIDDEN SOMEWHERE WITHIN
THE PAGES OF THIS BOOK.
CAN YOU FIND 11 HORSEHOES?

The Answers are at MimsHouse.com/aliens

PREVIEW
THE ALIENS, INC. SERIES
BOOK 3

KELL AND THE GIANTS

By Darcy Pattison

pictures by
Rich Davis

MIMS HOUSE / LITTLE ROCK, AR

CHAPTER 1

I bent over the giant state of Texas.

"Texas is so big," said Mrs. Crux the art teacher, "that I need three students to work together to paint it. Bree, Roman and Kell."

Ye-Haw! We are painting TEXAS!!

Our art class was painting a map of the United States on the basketball court. Alaska needed three people to paint it, too. Most kids were painting just one state. Some students had two small states to color. One student was painting five small states.

Roman East dabbed red paint on the south Texas beaches and said, "We need to plan my birthday party. I want a giant party."

I asked, "How big a party do you want?"

"No," Roman said. "Not a big party. A party about giants. You know, really tall people."

Roman was the tallest kid in third grade. I could understand why he was interested in giants.

I swiped red paint onto the Panhandle of north Texas.

Meanwhile, Bree Hendricks, my best friend, was painting red on the east side of Texas. She said, "No one knows anything about giants. Name one giant."

Roman said, "There was the one-eyed giant named Cyclops. Paul Bunyan was an American giant who lived in the forests and cut down giant trees. In the Bible, a boy named David killed a nine-foot giant named Goliath."

Bree giggled and said, "I just remembered a giant. There's the Jolly Green Giant who wears green underwear."

I frowned. I had only read about Atlas, the giant that is supposed to hold the world on his shoulders. Before my family crash-landed, we got a good look at Earth from space. There isn't a giant holding up the Earth. That Atlas story, it's just a folktale.

The art class was working outside in the wide-open spaces. But sure enough, a flying bug found me. It zoomed around my ears, and then flew high enough to be out of reach. Quick, I dropped to my knees and hissed at Bree, "What kind of bug?"

Her head circled, following the bug above my head. "It's a honeybee. It's OK. Don't smash it."

Slowly, I peeked upward and the bee dropped a couple inches closer. Terrified, I held very, very, very still. On Earth, there are more bugs than any other kind of animal. I don't like Earth bugs. You never knew when a bug might bite or sting you. This one had a black head, a golden body, and a stinger.

I waved at the honeybee to go away. It just circled my head again. I shivered and ducked.

Just then, Mrs. Lynx, the principal came  out of the school building and trotted over to us. She wore her toe shoes, so she ran very quietly. Running beside her was a dog about as tall as her knees. The dog had a brown head, ears and neck, but the back part of him was spotted. They stopped at the edge of the map and Mrs. Lynx said, "Sit."

The dog sat.

Meanwhile, the honeybee was gone, flying away when I wasn't looking. That didn't fool me. I knew it would be back.

"Be careful," Mrs. Crux said. "The paint is still wet."

Mrs. Lynx frowned. "Then how are they getting out of Texas?"

Bree and I backed into each other and then Roman bumped into us. We had painted ourselves into the very center of Texas. There was no way out!

Bree said, "It's OK. We can jump. Kell and I are good at hopscotch."

I groaned. I am an alien from the planet Bix. I can do telekinesis, which means I can move things with my mind. Bree wanted me to give her a boost when she jumped. But Mrs. Lynx is President of the S.A.C., the Society of Alien Chasers. If I helped Bree too much, Mrs. Lynx would suspect that I was an alien.

Still, we were trapped in Texas.

Mrs. Crux said, "Are you sure, mate, that you can jump far enough?" She is from Australia and says, "Mate," all the time.

Bree nodded and said, "I will jump on 3."

"1, 2, 3!" She leapt high—with a little help from a Bix alien—and landed on the tennis court away from the paint.

"You next," I told Roman.

"I can't jump that," Roman said. He has long legs and I thought he might even be able to take a giant step to get out of Texas. But he wouldn't try. Instead, he bent and leapt. He's so big and clumsy that he really needed a boost! He landed just outside Texas and fell into a heap.

Roman cried out, "What was that?" He twisted around to stare at me.

Oh, no! He must have felt me giving him a shove.

Quickly, Bree said, "You're a great jumper!"

He stood up and brushed off his shirt. Looking at the distance he had jumped, he stood a bit taller. "I'm a better jumper than I thought."

Now, I had to jump. I bent and leapt.

But right in mid-air—BZZZ! Three honeybees zipped around me. I slapped at them and forgot to do telekinesis. I fell onto south beaches of Texas

"Do you want me to give you jumping lessons?" Roman said. Smiling at his own joke, he held out a hand and I took it.

Roman pulled me up halfway, but then we got stuck. He pulled and I pulled, but I didn't go any farther. I was just hanging over Texas.

I pulled so hard that my arms were tired and shaky. Roman's arms were shaking, too.

And then, Roman dropped me!

"No!" I cried. Plop! I was back in the wet paint.

Roman swung his arms around to make them feel better. But the rest of the class just pointed and laughed. I dropped my face to my knees and groaned.

Roman bent down and this time grabbed my right hand with both of his hands. He jerked hard and I tumbled onto the basketball court. I pushed myself up and tried to stand.

"Look at his pants!"

"His butt is red!"

Across the giant map of the United States, kids laughed. I was so upset. To hide the red paint, I sat down on a blue bench.

Freddy Rubin yelled at me, "NO!"

What? Quick, I stood up and looked around.

Oh, no. The bench was splotched with red paint from

where I sat. It was times like this that I longed for my home planet of Bix. On Bix, red is the color of the sky. That red splotch on the blue bench left an ache, a longing to see the skies of Bix.

Mrs. Crux smiled at me, "Again, Mate?"

Sadly, I nodded. It was my 14th Accidental Art.

Mrs. Crux handed me a small paintbrush. "Why don't you just sign your name? Then I'll take a picture of it for the Accidental Art bulletin board. You can go to the office and call your mom to bring you new pants."

With a sigh, I took the brush and took some black paint from Aja. I painted my name on the bench beside my butt-print: Kell Smith. I may be an alien, but I'm not dumb. I made sure the name was smeared so badly that no one could read it.

Meanwhile, Mrs. Crux bent to pet Mrs. Lynx's dog. "When did you get her?"

Mrs. Lynx's eyes lit up. "My brother, Ernest, brought her yesterday. She's a German shorthaired pointer. He trained Gloria and she's the best alien pointer dog in the world."

"What does a pointer do?"

"When she smells an alien," Mrs. Lynx said, "she points and holds that point until I find the right person."

Oh, no! I thought. It was never safe with Mrs. Lynx around. She and the S.A.C. kept trying to catch an alien. Someday, she would catch my family and me.

Roman walked over to look at the dog. "May I pet her?"

"Yes," Mrs. Lynx said.

Roman squatted down and starting scratching the dog behind her ears.

Mrs. Lynx said, "Roman, I hear you're going to have a Giant birthday party. Aliens, Inc. does a great job with parties."

"Yes, ma'am," Roman said. "I hope we have stilts And maybe Big Foot can come."

I needed a Look-Up later list for a Giant party:

GIANT LOOK UP LATER LIST

1. What are stilts?
2. Who are Cyclops, Paul Bunyan, Goliath and Big Foot?

Just then, the bell rang and it was time to go inside. I would go by the office and call

Mom to bring me a change of clothes. Bree and I walked way around the other side of the basketball court to stay far away from the alien pointer dog named Gloria. But she was watching me. Gloria didn't fool me. She smelled me and sooner or later, she would point me out.

"Hey, I have a riddle for you," Bree said.

"OK."

"What is the best tasting throw-up?"

"Yuk," I said. "No throw up tastes good."

"Wrong," Bree said. "Honeybees eat nectar and then throw up honey."

That Bree. Earth girls are full of odd facts.

READ MORE ADVENTURES WITH KELL, BREE AND THE ALIENS, INC. GANG IN BOOK 3:

KELL AND THE GIANTS

Join our mailing list.

MimsHouse.com/newsletter/

Other Books in
The Aliens, Inc. Series

Book 1: Kell, the Alien
Book 2: Kell and the Horse Apple Parade
Book 3: Kell and the Giants
Book 4: Kell and the Detectives (2015)

Other Books by Darcy Pattison

Saucy and Bubba: A Hansel and Gretel Tale

The Girl, the Gypsy and the Gargyole

Vagabonds

Abayomi, the Brazilian Puma:

Wisdom, the Midway Albatross:

The Scary Slopes

Prairie Storms

Desert Baths

19 Girls and Me

Searching for Oliver K. Woodman

The Journey of Oliver K. Woodman

The River Dragon

ABOUT THE AUTHOR & ILLUSTRATOR

Translated into eight languages, children's book author DARCY PATTISON writes picture books, middle grade novels, and children's nonfiction. Previous titles include *The Journey of Oliver K. Woodman* (Harcourt), *Searching for Oliver K. Woodman* (Harcourt), *The Wayfinder* (Greenwillow), *19 Girls and Me* (Philomel), *Prairie Storms* (Sylvan Dell), *Desert Baths* (Desert Baths), and *Wisdom, the Midway Albatross* (Mims House.) Her work has been recognized by **starred reviews** in *Kirkus, BCCB,* and *PW. Desert Baths* was named a 2013 Outstanding Science Trade Book and the *Library Media Connection,* Editor's Choice. She is a member of the Society of Children's Bookwriters and Illustrators and the Author's Guild. For more information, see darcypattison.com.

RICH DAVIS, illustrator for the Aliens, Inc series has wondered, "What could be better than getting to do black and white cartoon work for a sci-fi easy reader?" Working on this book has been one big fun-making experience. Rich has also illustrated 12 other children's books, including beginning reader series, *Tiny the Big Dog* (Penguin). His joy is to help kids develop creatively and he has invented a simple drawing game (Pick and Draw.com) and an activities book as a fun tool that now have a following around the world. He frequently does programs at schools and libraries in order to draw with thousands of kids yearly. For him, it is a dream come true and he recognizes that the source is from God alone.